Snowshoe Trek to Otter River

Snowshoe Trek to Otter River

by David Budbill

pictures by Lorence F. Bjorklund

The Dial Press · New York

Library of Congress Cataloging in Publication Data
Budbill, David. Snowshoe trek to Otter River.
Summary: Three short stories relate the adventures
of twelve-year-old Daniel and his friend Seth while
camping in the woods alone and together.
[1. Camping—Fiction. 2. Nature—Fiction]
I. Bjorklund, Lorence F. II. Title.
PZ7.B8824Sn   [Fic]   75-27603
ISBN 0-8037-8055-9 ISBN 0-8037-8056-7 lib. bdg.

For Gene

Contents

Snowshoe Trek to
Otter River

Early in the morning
after Daniel finished breakfast, he took his backpack
off the wall and unpacked it. He had packed everything carefully last night, but now that it was time to
go, he had to be sure everything was there, ready, in
case he needed it. Daniel could see his mother moving about the kitchen, watching him out of the
corner of her eye. He knew she was laughing to

herself about the way he fussed over his equipment. But the gear was important. If he got caught out there in a blizzard, or if something happened to him and he couldn't get back, his life might depend on the few things he carried on his back.

He spread the backpack's contents on the kitchen floor. Nested cookpots: one 8-inch skillet with folding handle, one 6-inch plate, one quart pail with lid, a metal cup, a fork and spoon. His pocketknife would do the cutting. A bunch of waterproof matches wrapped in tinfoil. Two fire starters he had made by rolling paper tightly, tying it with string, and soaking it in hot paraffin. A compass, a hatchet, and a sleeping bag. Daniel cut three thick slices of his mother's homemade bread, buttered them, then took two chunks of bacon and three eggs from the refrigerator. He wrapped everything carefully and put it in the backpack with a bag of nuts and raisins, a little salt, a small jar of sugar, and a handful of tea in a small bag. As far as Daniel was concerned, bacon and eggs, bread, and tea was the perfect campfire lunch for a winter's day of snowshoeing.

Daniel was only twelve, but he knew a lot about getting along in the woods. His parents were dairy farmers. Although they lived surrounded by the wilderness, they never really were a part of it. But down the road from Daniel's house there was an old man, a Frenchman by the name of Mr. Bateau, who had come down from Canada years ago. Mr. Bateau was Daniel's favorite person. He was a man of the woods—a logger, a hunter, a fisherman, and a trapper. Mr. Bateau had taught Daniel all he knew about the wild world. He had shown him how to fish, build wilderness camps, identify wild flowers and animal tracks, how to talk to birds, call foxes, make coyotes howl. But most of all Mr. Bateau had given Daniel a love of the wilderness that drew Daniel out now into the white, cold world beyond his house.

Daniel's plan was to strike out across the high swamp behind his farm and continue down the mountain to Otter River in the valley below. Last summer he and his best friend, Seth, had built a lean-to on the far side of Otter River. Daniel planned to have his lunch at the camp, check the supplies they had stashed there, and return home before dark.

When the backpack was packed again, Daniel put on two pairs of heavy wool socks and pulled his rubber-bottom, leather-top winter boots over them. He wore long underwear and wool pants. Over a long-sleeved undershirt he wore a cotton shirt and over that a wool shirt and over that another, heavier wool shirt. If he got hot, he could peel off a layer or two, but he doubted he'd get hot. He looked out the window at the thermometer. It said ten degrees below zero. By noon it might be ten above.

He was ready. He slipped his backpack on, kissed his mother good-bye, and went onto the porch. He pulled his wool cap down over his ears, put on his mittens, picked up his snowshoes, and stepped out into the snow. He slipped his boots into the snowshoe harnesses and adjusted the bindings carefully.

It was a clear, bright, still day. The spruce and fir

trees on the horizon made a deep green band that separated the bright blue sky from the white, pure white earth. As Daniel struck out across the pasture behind the house, the cold air stung his face. It felt good. It was the perfect day for a hike.

Last night's snow had added six inches to the three feet already on the ground. Daniel knew the new snow meant animal tracks would be fresh. He'd do some tracking along the way.

Soon he was beyond the open fields and deep into the swamp. It was a different world, darker, quieter. The big spruce and fir trees covered up the sky. There was no sound. It was as if this swamp were a noiseless chamber. All Daniel could hear were his snowshoes, whispering, hissing as he moved along. He stopped. Listened. Now there was no sound at all. None. It was as if everything in the world were dead except for one boy who stood silent and alone, deep in a snowy evergreen swamp.

Suddenly, out of nowhere, the sound of galloping broke the silence. Daniel's heart jumped. He

crouched down and waited. Then, in a crash of twigs, a shower of snow, three deer burst into a clearing right in front of him—a buck, a doe, and last year's fawn. The three deer stopped. They stood silent in their tracks. Slowly the buck raised his head and sniffed the wind. He caught Daniel's scent. The buck gave a terrible snorting roar, stomped his foot, and away the three went in a muffled thunder of hooves, their sleek, brown bodies plowing through the snow. Daniel stood up and watched the three deer disappear into the dark trees. His heart was still pounding.

He came to a broad open place in the middle of the swamp. Beavers had dammed the swamp brook and made a pond. Daniel could see a large hump in the level snow near the dam. It was a beaver house. As Daniel crossed the pond, he thought about the beavers under all that snow and ice, lazing away the winter, safe in their underwater home. At this very moment there could be a beaver swimming only a few feet below his snowshoes.

9

When he reached the other side of the beaver pond, Daniel found some rabbit tracks. They weren't really made by a rabbit, even though everybody called them rabbits. They were made by a snowshoe hare, the kind that turns white in the winter and has big, webbed feet for getting around in deep snow. Daniel could tell from the size of the tracks that it was a young rabbit. He followed the tracks up the hill to a place where they stopped abruptly. Here there was a pool of frozen blood and beside the blood on either side, printed neatly in the snow, the marks of two large wings. Daniel knew what had happened.

The hare had been hopping along, when, out of the sky, swiftly, silently, a large hawk had dropped down, his wings set back, his large claws thrust out and down. Thud! Daniel could see the hawk's sharp claws sink into the rabbit's back. He could hear the rabbit scream as it died. Then the hawk beat his wings, leaving the prints there in the snow, and was away, up into the air with his breakfast.

Daniel felt sorry for the rabbit, but he knew this was the way the hawk ate, the way he stayed alive. Last fall Daniel had helped his father slaughter a pig so they could eat meat all winter. The hawk had slaughtered a rabbit so he could eat meat too. But Daniel couldn't help feeling sorry for the rabbit, just as he had felt sorry for the pig. He stood for a long time staring at the rabbit tracks that went nowhere, the frozen blood, the imprint of the hawk's wings. Then he pushed on.

He was out of the evergreen swamp now and starting down the mountain toward the river. Here the trees were all hardwoods, and the sun shone brightly through the bare branches. A chickadee scolded Daniel from a nearby tree.

Daniel saw tiny ruffed grouse tracks everywhere. The grouse had come to the hardwoods to eat the buds off birch trees. Suddenly there was a thundering rush, a wild flutter of wings. Daniel stopped. Grouse were flying everywhere, weaving crazily between the trees. One bird flew right at him. He threw his hands up in front of his face. Then the bird was gone.

Soon Daniel was down the mountain. Otter River was before him. He could see the snow-covered camp on the other side. He walked up and down the riverbank looking for a place to cross. Daniel knew that where the river ran still and deep the ice would be the thickest. There was a place like that about a hundred yards upstream, but the river looked safe here too and it wasn't quite so wide. Daniel took off his snowshoes. If he fell through with them on, his feet would be trapped under the ice. He stepped out onto the river and jumped up and down a couple of times. The ice was solid. He started across.

When he was almost to the far shore, he heard a loud, thundering crack begin near him and shoot up the river. Slowly, he began to sink. Then more and louder cracks. Then a deep, rumbling roar. He was going down! The whole river was opening up!

Daniel heaved his snowshoes onto the shore and grabbed for solid ice. His boots were full of water,

his legs numbed by the cold. Again and again he reached for the edge of solid ice. Each time the ice broke away and bobbed uselessly in front of him. Then his feet struck bottom. He stood waist deep in icy water. He could wade to shore. But there were great slabs of loose ice floating between him and the bank. When he tried to climb on top of them, they sank. When he tried to push them out of his way, they bumped into each other and blocked the way. He was trapped.

Daniel's mind raced. He had to think of something fast. In only a few minutes he would be so cold he'd faint. That would be the end. Quickly he took his pack off his back, undid the top, and grabbed his hatchet. He threw the pack up on the bank. Then, slowly, painfully, Daniel began chopping a channel through the slabs of ice toward the shore.

He reached the bank and pulled himself cold and numb out of the water. He was soaked. The instant his wet clothes met the cold air, they froze. His troubles had only begun.

By now his pants had frozen so hard he could barely bend his knees. He gathered up his snowshoes and pack and limped, stiff-legged, to his camp. Daniel was freezing, not just freezing cold, but actually freezing, freezing to death.

He took the small shovel he and Seth had stashed in the lean-to and cleaned the snow away from the fire pit. He broke an armful of dead branches off a hemlock tree for kindling, took one of the fire starters out of his pack, and lit a fire. He was glad now that last summer he and Seth had stacked dry wood next to the camp.

Soon the fire was burning. Daniel was sleepy and cold, so cold. All he wanted to do was lie down, but he knew he couldn't. Not yet.

He stuck two forked sticks in the snow, one on each side of the fire. Then he laid a long pole between the two sticks above the fire. He propped his snowshoes near the fire, crawled inside the lean-to, and spread his sleeping bag on the bare, dry ground inside the shelter. Then he put more wood on the fire.

When all this was done, he was ready to do the only thing left to do. He couldn't go home. It was too far away. He'd freeze before he got there. He couldn't call for help. There was no one for miles. He'd have to thaw and dry out before he could go any farther.

Although it was below zero, Daniel took off his clothes. He draped his pants and long underwear, socks, and mittens over the long pole. He hung a wool shirt on each snowshoe. He put his boots on a rock near the fire. The snow was so cold on his bare feet that it felt hot. When all his clothes were hung over the fire, he limped into the lean-to and climbed inside his sleeping bag. He shivered violently. He wanted to cry, but he was too cold. Slowly, very slowly, his body heat began to fill the sleeping bag. He began to warm up. He took the bag of nuts and raisins from his pack and ate. He could see his clothes dripping and steaming over the fire. Daniel was relaxed now. His eyes grew heavy. He fell asleep.

When Daniel woke up, the fire was down to coals. It was warm inside the bag. He had no idea how long he had slept. It may have been an hour or two. He got up and put more wood on the fire. He felt his clothes. They were dry, except for his boots. He got dressed. His clothes smelled like wood smoke. He hung his boots from the pole by their laces and began to fix lunch. He set the bacon to frying in the skillet and put some snow to melt in the quart pail for tea. Since snow water always tasted flat, he added a little salt to the melting snow.

When the water boiled, he added tea and put the pail on a rock at the edge of the fire. He reached into his backpack for the eggs. They were smashed. They must have broken when he threw the pack up on the bank. He dumped the slimy mixture into his metal plate and separated shell from egg as best he could. He took the cooked bacon out of the skillet and put the eggs in, scrambling them with his fork. They cooked quickly. Then he ate. It seemed to Daniel like the best meal he had ever eaten. Crisp bacon, eggs scrambled in bacon grease, good bread with lots of butter, and hot, sweet tea. It was good.

Daniel laughed to himself. Here he was, in the middle of winter, sitting by a fire, by a river he had just fallen into, eating lunch, thinking how good the tea was! It was hard to believe. A couple of hours ago he was almost dead. Now he sat comfortably, his feet warmed by the fire, almost as if nothing had happened.

When the last of the tea was gone, he put his boots on, cleaned and packed his gear, shoveled snow on the fire, rolled the sleeping bag, and started home. This time he headed upstream to where the river moved slowly and the ice was thick. Nobody ever crossed a frozen river more carefully than Daniel did that afternoon.

When he reached the other side, he noticed that

the sun was low in the southern sky. It got dark early this time of year, and home was a long way off. He'd have to travel to get there before dark.

He followed his own trail up through the hard-woods, over the brow of the mountain, and down into the swamp.

By the time he reached the other side of the bea-ver pond, the sun was almost down. It was dark in the thick trees of the swamp. Daniel had trouble finding his trail. It got darker and darker. He was hurrying now, and, although it was growing colder, he was sweating. Then out of the darkening sky fear dropped down and seized him. He had gotten off the trail. He was lost.

Daniel was running. He had to find his old trail and fast. But the faster he moved, the more confused he got. Then he stopped. He found a log sticking up above the snow, brushed the snow off its top, and sat down. He knew that to get panicky when lost was the worst thing that could happen. He took the bag of nuts and raisins from his pack and ate a handful. He would sit here until he quieted down and decided what to do. But it was hard. He had to force himself to sit on that log. Something inside urged him to get up and run. It didn't matter where, just run! He fought the urge with all the strength he had.

Then he heard the soft rustle of wings. A large white bird floated silently into a tree above him. It was a snowy owl. It seemed to Daniel like a ghost. Its fierce yellow eyes shot through him like needles. Why did that bird sit there, staring? What did it want? Daniel couldn't stand it. He jumped up, made a snowball, and threw it at the owl. The snowball almost hit the owl, but the owl didn't move. He sat there, staring, as if to say, "I'm not the one who is afraid." Then, as if nothing had happened, the snowy owl rolled backward off the branch and disappeared without a sound into the dark trees.

The owl, the noiseless chamber of a forest, the darkness, frightened Daniel more than falling in the river. When he had gone down in the river, he

knew what he had to do to save himself. The only question was whether he could do it. But here, in this wild place, there was something unknown, something strange. He felt out of place, alone, deserted. It seemed as if even the trees around him were about to grab him, take him off somewhere, deeper into the swamp, where he would be lost forever.

He decided what to do. He would get up, calmly, and follow his tracks back to where he lost the trail. He'd get back on the trail and go home. It was hard to go back, but he had to do it.

When he found the trail again, he moved along it slowly. It was so dark now he couldn't afford to get lost again. At last, after what seemed like hours, he found himself standing at the edge of a broad, open field. At the far end of the field he could see his house. The kitchen window glowed warm and orange in the dusky evening light. He struck off across the meadow toward the lighted window.

Daniel took off his snowshoes and stuck them in

the snow in front of the house. He dumped his back-pack on the porch and stepped into the bright, warm kitchen. His parents were fixing supper.

"Well, where have you been? We were begin-ning to worry," his father said.

"The hike took longer than I thought."

"How was it?" his mother asked.

"It was okay."

"Didn't you have any fantastic adventures?"

Daniel looked at his mother and smiled. He said, "No, not today."

Float Down
the Tamarack

Daniel was finishing breakfast when Seth stepped into the kitchen. It was seven o'clock. The sun had already climbed over Black Spruce Mountain. The ravens were croaking over the swamp as they did every sunny morning. The water was still high in Tamarack Brook. It was the perfect day for the boys' plan: a trip by canoe down the Tamarack into the wild and lonely heart of Bear Swamp.

"Ready?" Seth questioned.

"Just about," Daniel replied through a mouthful of toast and jam.

"Well, come on! It's late. Got the gear together?"

"It's in the canoe."

"Let's go!"

"Okay," Daniel said, heading for the door.

It was the first of June, and here in the north spring had only just begun. The apple trees were about to blossom; the hardwood leaves were still pale and new. There had been a light frost that morning, and where the sun had not yet fallen, the grass was white.

The warmth of the kitchen didn't follow the boys into the dank chill of the woodshed. Their light wool jackets felt good. In the woodshed's half-light the boys inspected the equipment in the canoe: two paddles, a set of nested cookpots, two fishing rods and tackle, two canvas creels, and a can of worms. In a small backpack, a waterproof bag held some bacon, a small bag of tea, some cornmeal, and bread and butter. The boys planned to cook their lunch—fresh-caught trout, bread and butter, bacon, tea—somewhere in the middle of the swamp. When they were satisfied everything was in order, they hauled the canoe out of the shed and dragged it across the pasture toward a small bridge that crossed the brook a few hundred yards below the house.

As they neared the brook, they heard, over the quiet rush of water, a snapping sound. There, on the far bank, a mother mink, humped up like a cat, hissed and spat at the boys as if she were ten feet tall. Seth and Daniel put the canoe down quietly and backed away down the road a little. They knew the mink had young somewhere near, and, until she had time to get her babies to safety, she would be trouble. The boys waited. Soon the mink disappeared, taking her unseen young with her somewhere away from these huge, two-footed strangers.

When the mink was gone, the boys climbed down the bank and put the canoe in a few feet downstream from the bridge, where a gravel bar gave them easy access to the brook. At this point Tamarack Brook was a small stream, not more than eight feet wide, choked with alders on both sides.

Before they got into the canoe, Seth took a small bottle of black liquid from his shirt pocket and poured some of the thick, oily contents into the palm of one hand. He rubbed it over his hands and arms, his face and neck. He took a bandana from his pocket, daubed it in the liquid, and tied it around his neck. He took off his cap and poured some of the liquid onto the bill. Then Daniel took the bottle and did the same. When they were done, their hands and faces glistened darkly in the sun.

It was fly dope, but not just any fly dope. This was a vile-smelling concoction known in these parts for a hundred years, a witches' brew, whipped up out of pine tar and citronella. It was strong stuff, and it had to be. Early June was a buggy time. The air was full of black flies, gnats, no-see-ums, and mosquitoes. Without the fly dope and plenty of it, the boys wouldn't get a hundred feet into the swamp before they were eaten alive.

"If the wind's right, they'll smell us all the way back to the house!" Daniel said proudly. The boys loved the stink. It meant adventure. It meant wilderness.

They were ready. It would be a rough trip and the boys knew it, but what led them on was the promise of the huge beaver pond at the swamp's center and the trout Mr. Bateau said lived there.

The idea for the trip had come one cold and snowy night last winter when Seth and his parents and Mr. Bateau were visiting at Daniel's house. That night, as everyone sat in the kitchen drinking coffee and eating homemade doughnuts, Mr. Bateau got to telling stories about the old days when he was logging the edges of Bear Swamp. He told a story about finding a huge beaver pond in the middle of the swamp. "That was the biggest beaver dam I ever see. I fish there once too and I catch the speckled trout. One from here to here!" He ran his finger from his elbow to his fingertips. "Big as my arm!"

Mr. Bateau was a great storyteller, but truth was never one of his greatest concerns. Everyone loved to listen to him talk, but no one really believed his stories, especially one about an eighteen-inch trout —no one, that is, except Seth and Daniel.

"Big fish in there. And no fishermans go there, too hard to get to. The alders too thick; the grass she too high and that muddy muck, bah gosh, that terrible. Fishermans ask me once if he sink up to his knees in that muddy muck. I say yes you do, if you walking on your head! The only way you get there is in spring when the water is high, you take canoe down the brook, right through the alders. You be rugged man to get there!"

That winter evening the boys decided. They could do it and they would, come spring.

As they pushed off from the gravel bar, the boys realized Mr. Bateau hadn't been kidding. They could see the brook weave its narrow, twisted way through the knotted tangle of alders and marsh grass. It was impossible to paddle the canoe. The brush was too thick, the stream too crooked and, in spots, too shallow. They had to use their paddles as poles to push the canoe along.

They banged from one bank to the other, bumped against dead trees and stumps, ran aground over and over again on sand and gravel bars. By the time they had gone less than a hundred yards, both boys were soaked with sweat, even though they had long since taken off their jackets.

Soon the alders were so thick and low across the stream that they had to lie down in the canoe and pull themselves along by grabbing low-hanging branches. In spite of what Mr. Bateau had said, the boys had had dreams of paddling quietly along the stream, fishing for trout. This was nothing like that. This was work. The branches slapped them across the face and caught in their clothes. The canoe began to fill with broken twigs, dead grass, and leaves. There were places where it took all the strength the two boys had to pull themselves and the canoe through the tangle of stumps and branches. The canoe squeaked and screamed as they yanked it through the debris. They were trying to be careful. All they needed now was a puncture. A canoe full of water wouldn't be much good, and with no canoe they'd be trapped.

"If we ever make it through this mess, there better be some trout!" Seth said.

Just as the boys thought they might be through the worst of the alder tangle, they ran headlong into an abandoned beaver dam. There was no way they could pull themselves across. They would have to climb out into the icy water and haul the canoe over. The water was cold! Only a couple of weeks ago it had still been skinned with ice. By the time the boys dragged the canoe over the dam and got back in, their feet and legs were numb. Now mud and icy water mingled with the twigs, grass, and leaves that littered the bottom of the canoe.

"Seth, why don't you put that backpack on? It's getting wet," Daniel said.

Seth slipped the cold and dripping backpack over his shoulders, shivered a little, and they pushed on.

Slowly the alders began to thin out. Then there weren't any branches anywhere. The marsh grass came right down to the brook. The brook flowed broad and quiet. The boys sat up for the first time and actually paddled the canoe.

They moved quietly now; their paddles stroked the water silently. Then suddenly a loud, sharp *kuck-kuck-kutck!* shattered the stillness. Out of a dead tree standing near the stream bank a huge pileated woodpecker, big as a crow, flew away in alarm, his strong wings slicing the morning air. The boys could see in the bare tree the large oblong holes the woodpecker had cut in search of insects. Some of the holes were two feet long and six inches deep. As the woodpecker flew away, his bright red crested head, his black-and-white feathers, his strong, undulating flight, sent shivers of excitement down the boys' spines.

A little farther downstream, where the banks

were high, there was a smooth, wet groove in the clay bank. It was an otter slide, a place where the big minklike animals came to play, to slide down the slippery clay and into the brook over and over again, just for the joy of it.

"Boy! I'd like to see an otter," Seth said. "I've never seen one. Have you?"

"Nope. I would too, but I bet we won't today. That woodpecker told the otters we were coming. We may not see them, but I bet they see us."

As the boys made their way easily downstream, Daniel exclaimed, "Now this is more like it!"

"Well, don't get your hopes up," Seth said. "Look ahead." About a hundred yards downstream the open place ended abruptly in another incredible tangle of alders.

If their first stretch of rough going had been a bad dream, this was a nightmare. Not only were the alders thicker, but there were old beaver dams every few feet. The boys were out of the canoe more than in it. For some stretches they had to walk through the stream pulling the canoe behind them, dragging it over the stumps and through the branches.

Once, after they had climbed back into the canoe, the stream got so shallow they had to get out again. Daniel swung his leg over the edge of the canoe and stepped into the few inches of water. He began to sink. He kept sinking until he was stuck in gray-black swamp muck almost to his chest.

Seth sat in the canoe and laughed.

"Come on, Seth! Help me out of here!"

With great tugging and pulling, grunting and groaning, Seth got his soggy, half-frozen, muck-covered friend back into the canoe. They headed for shore, climbed the bank, dragged the canoe up, and portaged around the shallow place.

The alders began thinning out again. Then it happened. All of a sudden the alders were gone, and as far as they could see ahead of them, the brook wound broad and quiet through a flat plain of old stumps and marsh grass. Far at the other end, almost half a mile ahead, was a huge beaver pond, its smooth surface glittering in the sun, and at the far end of the pond the boys could see the dam, that half-moon miracle of woven birch and alder branches.

In spite of the cuts on their faces, the mud and muck, the heat and cold, the boys were laughing. "He was right! Mr. Bateau was right! There it is! Big as a lake!"

The boys sat in the canoe and glided along the broad stream. It was as if they had come through a terrible storm and this was the eye, the still center. As they moved along, the only sound they heard was the quiet dip of their paddles.

As Seth and Daniel rounded a small bend, six black ducks rose in a splashing cackle in front of them. The ducks climbed about a hundred feet, then banked to the right as if they were one bird, made a slow turn over the broad swamp, and headed upstream toward the road. The boys watched their round, graceful bodies, their quick wings, their long necks stuck straight out in front of them. They listened to their chattering quacks, that strange duck talk they couldn't understand.

Now for the first time the boys didn't have to struggle against the swamp. They could look around, and what they saw amazed them. Both boys lived in wild country, but this place made their farms, their fields, seem tame by comparison. Here there was no sign of humanity—no tin cans, no power lines, nothing. It was as if human beings had never been here before, as if they were the first ones ever to see this place.

For more than a hundred yards on either side of the brook the dead, brown marsh grass stretched flat away through a maze of black stumps. Where the swamp stopped, the trees began, huge spruce and fir trees, their deep-green, pointed spears jabbing the delicate-blue, cloud-white sky. Seth and Daniel had entered another world, a world hidden from the rest by a great, round wall of trees. It was a wild and secret place.

As the boys floated noiselessly, they felt out of place. They were aware, somewhere inside, that

40

they were strangers here. This was a world of wild creatures, of water, grass, and trees, a world that neither knew nor cared for people. It was an exciting place to be, and also a little frightening.

Lost as they were in their thoughts, neither boy saw the furry creature swimming toward the canoe. When the beast was almost even with them, Seth whispered, "Daniel! Don't move. Look left."

Alongside the canoe a big beaver swam easily upstream. He was so close, the boys could have reached out and touched him. They could see his dark eyes blinking in the canoe's wake, his thick, almost black, soaking fur, and his huge orange teeth. Wherever he was going, he was in no hurry. He seemed totally unconcerned with the boys' presence. Then he ducked quietly under the water's skin, his big, hairless tail rising in a quick swish, and was gone.

At that moment Daniel accidentally bumped the side of the canoe with his paddle, and the noise echoed across the swamp. Suddenly there was a

great crack and then a number of splashes. Another beaver had seen the boys; he had slapped a warning with his flat tail across the water, and all the other beavers in the pond immediately headed for the safety of their underwater home. It was the last the boys would see of beaver that day.

The boys had almost forgotten they had come to fish. But now the broad, deep water made them think of trout, big trout. They paddled quickly across the pond, beached the canoe at the beaver dam, and got out. Their legs were stiff. They brushed off the sandy swamp muck, applied a new layer of fly dope, got their fishing tackle ready, and climbed back into the canoe.

The beaver house stood about a hundred feet out in the pond from the dam. The boys knew the water would be deepest between the house and the dam. Quietly now they positioned the canoe over the deep water, baited their hooks, and cast them across the water. Daniel's worm hadn't sunk six inches when he had a strike! Then Seth did too. All the trouble, all the struggle had been worth it for this moment! The pond was alive with trout, or so they thought. As Daniel lifted his fish into the canoe he cried, "Oh! No! Dace." Seth had the same disappointing fish on his line.

Black-nosed dace are large members of the minnow family, a food fish for trout. Where there are dace, there are almost always trout, but the dace always get to the bait first.

The boys were disgusted. All this way, all that trouble, and for what? A bunch of dace, something they could catch anywhere. They tried again, and again they caught dace. Something had to be done; some way had to be found to get around the dace and down to the trout. That was it! Down. Maybe the trout were under the dace, in the deeper water. The boys added lead weights to their lines about a foot above the hooks.

The worms sank rapidly now, all the way to the bottom, through almost six feet of water. In that much water there could be big trout. Nothing. The boys sat waiting, floating on the quiet skin of water. Waiting. Waiting. Then slowly, very slowly, Daniel's line began to move away from the canoe, then back, then away again. Something was down there, down in that dark water; something was on! Daniel set the hook. It was a small fish, but Daniel didn't care; he wanted to know what kind. Slowly, carefully he brought it to the top, pulling gently against the fish's desperate struggle to get free. Trout!

Again and again their baits sank to the bottom and hooked trout. There wasn't much size to the fish, all of them between six and eight inches, but that was the best size for eating. They would be perfect for lunch.

Lunch. In the excitement the boys had almost forgotten how hungry they were, but now their stomachs demanded attention.

"Let's bring in our lines and go cook lunch," Daniel said. "We've got eight. That's plenty."

"Good idea. I'm starved!"

Daniel stowed his rod in the canoe and got ready to paddle to the dam. "What's the matter, Seth?" Seth was yanking on his line.

"I'm hung up, I guess. Must have hooked a stump or something. Only it moves a little when I pull hard on it."

"Probably you're caught on a limb and it gives a little."

Daniel maneuvered the canoe around to the other side of the snag so Seth could get a better angle to free himself. Seth pulled. Again the snag moved.

"It's no use," Seth said. "I'll have to break my line."

Then the snag moved again and Seth was free, or so he thought. When he had his bait almost to the surface, his reel began to spin, and the line raced away from the canoe! In the next instant a huge trout broke the water, leaped into the air, turned a somersault, and disappeared again into the pond.

"Yeow!" Seth shouted. "That's no snag!"

The battle was on. The big trout raced from one

side of the pond to the other. He leaped into the air. He dove down to the bottom. He raced toward the canoe, then away, then back again.

"We're in trouble!" Daniel shouted. "We didn't bring a net! We'll never get him over the edge of the canoe without one! He'll break your line!"

"What'll we do?" Seth was almost in tears. This was the one they had been waiting for. He had to have him.

"I'll try to get us to the dam. It's our only chance. You stay with him."

Their only hope of landing a fish this big without a net was to play him until he was exhausted, then drag him ashore onto the beaver dam. Daniel slowly, carefully, moved the canoe toward the shore. When they reached the dam, both boys got out, and Seth continued struggling with his fish.

After almost half an hour, the big trout flopped helplessly as Seth reached down through the shallow water and grabbed twenty inches of beautiful, speckled muscle and fight.

"Big as my arm!" Seth shouted.

"Bigger," Daniel said. "Let's have lunch."

"Are you kidding? Let's go find another one of these!"

"Come on. Let's eat. I'm starved." Daniel was a little jealous, even a little mad. He wished he'd been the one to catch the big trout.

As they got their cooking gear together, all Seth could say was, "What a battle! What a fish! Did you see the way he jumped? Did you see it?"

And all Daniel could say was, "Yeah. Yeah. I saw it."

A small brook entered the beaver pond near the dam. The boys could see where it wound its way down through the big spruce and fir trees and into the swamp. The water in the pond was brown from silt and pollen. A good pail of tea needed clear water, so the boys worked their way up the brook, out of the swamp, and into the cool shade of the evergreen trees. They found a place where there was a broad, clean gravel bar, the perfect spot for a safe fire. Here the brook bubbled quiet and clear over clean stones.

As Daniel arranged stones for a fireplace, Seth went in search of dead, dry wood. He was still talking to himself about his big trout. When the fire was going, Daniel took the quart pail from the nested cookpots, filled it with water from the brook, and set it to boiling over the fire; then he gutted the eight small trout, rinsed them in the brook, and laid them aside on a smooth flat stone. Seth took the frying pan from the backpack and began frying bacon. The bacon would be good between bread and butter, and a little of the leftover grease was just what was needed for frying the trout. When the bacon was cooked, Daniel covered each trout with cornmeal. The meal would make a crisp, delicious crust on the fried fish.

Daniel spit into the skillet. When the small drops of spittle jumped and danced across the surface of the pan, he knew the temperature was right for frying. After the water boiled, Seth dumped in the tea and set the pail to the side of the fire where it would stay warm but not boil.

Now the boys sat back, relaxed, and ate. This was a still, peaceful place. The only sounds were the gentle gurgle of the brook, the wind moving easily through the tops of the big trees, and an occasional chickadee who sang to interrupt the noontime quiet. And such smells: the sweet, delicate summertime odor of spruce and fir, the smell of woodsmoke, the smell of bacon and trout frying. There couldn't be a better way to have lunch.

Daniel broke a piece of bread from his sandwich and laid it on a large boulder on the other side of the stream. Before long a chipmunk appeared. It crept cautiously toward the bread and, seeing no enemies near, sat up on its back legs and ate.

When lunch was done, the boys stretched out against a large rock, sipped the last of their tea, and stared blankly through the deep, cool woods.

"You know what?" Seth said. "We ought to build another camp right here, like the one on Otter

River. We could hike down here from the upper crossroads, stay a day or two, fish the pond, then move on down to the river camp."

"Yeah, that'd be good," Daniel replied lazily. "We could be gone three or four days. It would be a real test of how good we were in the woods."

The boys dreamed on. They made plans. Dreaming about things was as much fun as doing them—in fact, often it was more fun. In dreams there never seemed to be bugs or mud. There were never any mishaps or mistakes, everything went just right. The boys were silent for a long time.

"Hey!" Seth shouted. "We could sit here all day. But if we want another monster, we'd better get going."

They poured water on the fire, then held the ashes in their hands to make sure they were cold. They washed the pots in the stream, packed the backpack, and headed toward the canoe.

As the boys moved out of the cool woods, the swamp's steaming midday heat hit them like a slap across the face. The bright light hurt their eyes. But the thought of another monster trout made them forget their discomfort, and they were soon back in the canoe baiting their hooks.

Seth and Daniel fished hard that afternoon, and each boy caught his legal limit of twelve trout. But they never again had the thrill of another monster. The sun began to sink. It was time to go, but Seth kept saying, "One more try! One more try!"

Finally the threat of darkness and the thought of the long struggle back drove the boys to put away their gear and head upstream. The trip out of the swamp was worse than the trip in, but the boys didn't mind. They had what they had come for, a story and a memory.

When they reached the road, it was almost dark. The six black ducks they had seen earlier that day whistled low over their heads. They were headed straight for the wild and secret innards of the swamp. The ducks and the boys were heading in opposite directions, but they were both going home.

The Last Days of
Brightness

The partridge rose in a shower of leaves, a thundering rush, a wild flutter of wings, and dove crazily through the naked branches of a maple tree. October. One of those perfect October days, crisp and cool as a carrot, the sky, a cloudless, turquoise blue.

It wouldn't be long now before the days of color and light gave way to cold November rain, then

sleet and rain, then snow, layer on layer, foot on top
of foot, six months of freeze. But not yet. These
were the last days of brightness and Seth meant to
use them well. He had gotten up before the sun, had
a light breakfast and packed his gear. He had gone
down to the barn where his parents were already
doing the morning milking and said good-bye. Then
he headed out. He was anxious to get going. This
would probably be his last chance for a good hike
on bare ground. Besides, this trip was a test for Seth.
Not long ago he and Daniel had had an argument
about staying the night alone in the woods. Daniel
had dared him to do it. Now Seth was going to try.

Ever since Seth could remember, he had enjoyed
being by himself. He always felt good about himself when he was alone. He had spent the night
alone out behind the house many times. But Daniel
claimed it was a lot different sleeping out behind the
house and sleeping out at the pond camp deep in the
wild and lonely innards of Bear Swamp. Seth wasn't

so sure. Well, by tomorrow morning he'd know. He wasn't worried. He could do it. At least he thought he could.

Seth watched the partridge set its wings and glide, tilting this way and that, through the hardwood trees. Then the bird disappeared into the dark cedars of the swamp.

There had been a hard frost the night before and, although the sun was up, here in the woods, where there were shadows, the ground was still white.

Autumn was almost over. All the hardwood leaves were down except the brown beech leaves, which would hang on all winter, crackling and rasping in the wind. The needles on the tamarack trees were turning yellow, getting ready to fall. All the color that had dressed the woods brightly just a week ago now lay ruined and brown on the forest floor. As far as Seth was concerned, this was the most beautiful time of the year. It was a quiet time, a time of clarity and stillness.

Above him two long Vs of geese heading south barked and honked across the sky. Their wild, mysterious cries saddened Seth. This was the time of leaving. There would be a long, merciless winter before he heard that sound again. Now as Seth moved quietly through the woods, he felt lonely, alone.

Seth's plan was to hike up Raven Hill to Isaiah Morey's deserted sugarhouse, have a look around, then move across the base of Dunn Hill and head down Walker Brook toward the camp he and Daniel had built last summer on the edge of Bear Swamp. He'd spend the night at the camp and come home in the morning—that is, if he could stand it there, all night, alone.

In his backpack he had his cookpots, food for three meals, a ground cloth, his sleeping bag, and a folding saw. Seth always carried a saw instead of a hatchet and a belt knife instead of a pocketknife.

Seth moved through a hardwood grove, his feet wading in the noisy, sun-dried leaves. Then he

found the hint of an old logging road, or maybe a sugar road that might take him to Isaiah Morey's sugarhouse.

It was fun to find old roads in the woods. Even after they had been unused for fifty or seventy-five years, their imprint remained. There was always that slight two-track depression, the result of years of sugar sleds and the big machines loggers use. Even when there were trees growing in the middle of the road, you could still find the road print winding through the woods. As Seth walked along the old road, he wondered about the last wagon to creak and groan here; he wondered about the first.

Then, ahead of him, Seth could see the telltale sign of something human. A sharp angular line interrupted the trees. Maybe it was the angle of a roof. He couldn't tell for sure from where he was, but he did know that whatever it was, it was human. Seth knew, as all backwoods children do, that everything in the natural world is rounded, tree trunks and branches, puff balls and leaves, rain drops and birds, the sun and the moon, the hills—not perfect circles but rounded. His eye, without his knowing, without his being able to talk about it, had been trained to know that. Now as he got closer, he could see that it *was* a roof, the roof of Mr. Morey's sugarhouse.

He left the trees and pushed through a patch of raspberries and hardhack. Then he stood at the gaping, open side of the ruined building.

He stepped over a hand-hewn beam and into the ruin. All the sugaring equipment was gone. There was nothing useful left. Only a few sap buckets and lids littered the floor. In a darkened corner a broken table and chair tilted in a rubble of boards and tin. An old ladder made from poles leaned up against the wall. The mark of porcupines was everywhere, boards and beams gnawed away and those round, fibrous pellets—porcupine droppings. As Seth moved across the rotten floor, it creaked and sagged under his weight.

Off the back of the sugarhouse there was a shed.

The door into it hung in its frame by one hinge. Seth opened it slowly, carefully. Inside were a rusted, broken cast-iron cookstove and a cot. Someone had lived here during sugaring. The remains of what used to be a straw mattress lay in a filthy pile on the floor. On the wall was an old coat. Seth could see where a chipmunk had nested in its pocket.

Although Seth knew he was alone, it seemed almost as if he were being watched, as if the ghosts of those who worked here long ago, long before even his parents were born, still hovered in the air. It wasn't frightening exactly, just odd. Seth knew the ghosts meant him no harm. It was just that the place still seemed to belong to them, even after all these years. It made Seth feel like an intruder.

Then he found some writing on the sagging door. He could barely make it out: "Isaiah Morey . . . 1910 . . . May God . . ."

As Seth moved from the shed back into the darkened sugarhouse, his foot bumped something. He looked down. There, rolled over on its back, its four feet sticking straight up, lay a porcupine, stiff in death.

Out in the sun again, Seth found the sugar road and pushed on. He was hungry. He found a sunny place near a beech tree where a deer had pawed away the leaves looking for nuts. He eased his backpack off, sat down, and had his lunch.

He ate a peanut butter sandwich, some fresh carrots, and a tomato he'd snitched from the windowsill that morning. It was the last tomato, the end of summer. Then he propped his backpack behind his head, stretched himself out on the dry leaves, and ate a couple of cookies.

A red squirrel bounced and chattered across a branch just above his head. The midday sun was warm. A light breeze rattled through the trees and the woods smelled of that delicious, sweet odor of dying leaves. Seth fell asleep.

"Hello!"

"What!" Seth sat up with a frightened start. There was a man standing over him.

"You all right?"

"Ah . . . yeah . . . sure."

The man carried a shotgun, and Seth could see a partridge tail sticking out of his hunting vest.

"Could I see 'em?"

The man laid the limp bodies of two ruffed grouse on the ground.

"Would you like a tail feather for your hat?"

"Sure!"

Seth slipped the beautiful, dark brown feather with light brown bands into the ribbon on his red felt hat.

"Thanks a lot."

"That's okay," the man said, as he moved away.

For a moment Seth wanted to call the stranger back so they could talk. He suddenly realized that the words he'd said to the stranger were the first words he'd spoken all day. It was good to hear his own voice, good to hear another human voice. But Seth didn't call him back. Instead he sat and watched

the stranger move down the sugar road and disappear into the trees.

Seth looked at the feather in his hat. It looked
good. He'd seen a picture once, in a book, of an old
Indian man with a red felt hat, a crusher, just like
his, with a partridge feather in it.

Seth slipped his pack on and headed down around
the base of Dunn Hill. He paused at a little brook,
had a drink, and rested. By the looks of the tracks a
big buck deer had stopped here for a drink the night
before.

If Seth had it figured right, he should head west
and cross Walker Brook somewhere near its source.

As the sunny hardwood knoll gave way to a stand
of dark spruce and fir, Seth could see ahead of him a
wet, open place in the softwoods, a beaver meadow,
an ancient beaver pond now filled with silt and
growing back to trees. He circled the wet place,
found the small trickle of water that was its outlet,
and headed downhill. Seth thought this must be the

headwaters of Walker Brook.

As he descended the mountainside, the brook slowly grew. Springs and rills met the brook all along the hillside. At first the brook spoke only now and then, in a whispering trickle. But by the time Seth crossed the upper crossroads, ambled with the brook through a deserted pasture, and headed toward the swamp, it bounced over rocks and worn ledges, falling over itself, down waterfalls, roaring to itself as it grew.

In the woods again, the brook raced through a deep ravine. At one point Seth stood on top of a cliff as high as a house and looked down over the hissing water to where it fell roaring on the boulders below. He tried not to think about falling.

Carefully Seth climbed from boulder to ledge to boulder again, down toward the swamp. Every footrest, every handhold had to be right, exactly right. Slowly, slowly, down he climbed.

When he reached the bottom of the falls, he noticed something white lying in a pool of deep green, swirling water. He rolled up his sleeve and reached down through the icy water. A deer skull. Last spring, probably, a young deer weak from the long, starving winter, had tried to cross the swollen brook somewhere above the falls. The fast water had taken it and dashed it mercilessly on these rocks. Seth put the skull in his backpack, looked up toward the top of the falls far above him, and shuddered quietly to himself. He moved on.

Now in the deep softwoods on the edge of the swamp Seth could see the lean-to he and Daniel had built last summer.

The camp was in pretty good shape. A few minor repairs, a little cleaning up, and everything would be tidy. Seth dumped his backpack on the ground and set to work. He uncovered the salt and sugar he and Daniel had sealed tight in canning jars and stashed there during the summer. They had also left a coffee-can-and-coat-hanger tea pail on a nail. There was a mouse nest in it.

The stone fireplace they'd built on a sandbar in

the brook was the perfect place to cook this time of year. October was a dry time, the fire season. A fire on a sandbar was safe. Seth would keep the fire small, as he always did, a cooking fire.

After he made the few necessary repairs and gathered wood for the fire, he walked down the brook to where it entered the swamp, to the beaver dam where he and Daniel had fished last spring.

As he walked out on the beaver dam, a great blue heron rose awkwardly out of the cattails and croaked away over the treetops.

"Sorry," Seth said, as the bird disappeared.

Then he saw a beaver surface near the beaver-house at the center of the pond. Maybe it was the same beaver that swam past the canoe last spring. It was like seeing an old friend.

Seth stood on the beaver dam remembering last spring's fishing trip, remembering the big trout. Then he wandered back to camp, poking here and there along the way. It was good to be back.

He took the ground cloth from his backpack

and spread it out inside the lean-to. Then he unrolled his sleeping bag. He reached inside his backpack for his cookpots and food. He pawed around. He opened the bag wider and looked inside. They weren't there. How could that be? He remembered checking twice, as he always did, when he packed. He was sure he had put them in. Or at least he thought he was sure.

Seth began talking to himself. "Idiot! All the times you've gone camping, you've never done this! And now, when you're out here in this forsaken place overnight alone for the first time . . ."

Seth was more irritated than frightened. He knew he could find something to eat in the woods, but it was getting late and he was hungry and tired.

He couldn't have forgotten the gear completely; maybe he left it up near the sugarhouse where he had lunch. That was probably it, but a lot of good it did him. The sugarhouse was twice as far as home. He couldn't get to either before dark.

The Last Days of Brightness

There was no one to take the blame, no one but himself, and no point in any more moaning. He'd made a mistake, and he'd have to live with it. But he'd have to live with it quickly. It was getting dark.

He slipped his empty backpack on and headed for the swamp. He remembered that last spring he'd smelled mint and wintergreen in the swamp. That would make good tea. And there were cattails. Cattail roots were good boiled, sort of like potatoes.

Seth reached the spot where the heron had been and pulled up about a dozen cattails, cut off their knobby, brown roots with his belt knife, and put them in his pack. Then, after wandering around a bit, he noticed a familiar-looking bush with glossy, round, deep-green leaves on the downstream side of the beaver dam. He picked a leaf, crushed it between his fingers, and sniffed. Wintergreen. It smelled just like chewing gum, only stronger, better. He picked a good handful and stuffed it in his shirt pocket.

Seth continued across the beaver dam and foraged on the far side of the pond. Then on a small hummock he saw something else he recognized. Cranberries. They would be much too bitter to eat alone, but if he could find the last of some blackberries or raspberries somewhere, the two together with some sugar would be delicious.

Finding blackberries or raspberries wasn't as easy as Seth had imagined, and he was not the first one to come upon the blackberries he finally found. The bushes were beaten down, their stalks stripped of leaves as well as berries. It was the sure sign of a bear. Bears weren't too dainty when they ate berries. There were only a few left. They were old and dry, but they would do. Seth picked them carefully, wondering how a bear could stand all those thorns in its paws and mouth.

Wintergreen for tea, cranberries and blackberries for dessert, cattail roots for potatoes—too bad he didn't have some meat. Then it dawned on him.

In his first-aid kit he always carried a few yards of
fishing line and a couple of hooks. Seth cut an alder
branch and made a crude fishing pole. Now the only
thing between him and a couple of trout was some
bait. With his belt knife he began digging in a rotten
log. Nothing. Then in another log and another. Still
nothing. Finally he found what he was looking for:
grubs, tiny, white, wormlike creatures, with little
brown, ugly heads, about the size of his thumbnail.
They were great trout bait. But he had only two. If
he was careful, two grubs could mean two trout.
They did.

Seth built a fire, then washed the tea pail and
peeled the cattail roots. After the fire had settled to
coals and the cattail roots were boiling in their water, Seth gutted the two trout and skewered them on
a green, forked stick. He roasted them slowly, turning them again and again over the hot coals. When
the trout curled and began to fall from the stick, he
ate.

Seth had forgotten his anger. He was so involved in what he was doing that he hadn't noticed the sun had slipped behind the mountains. Now it was rapidly growing dark. He put some wood on the fire and let it grow a little.

He took off his boots and crawled inside the lean-to. He propped his head on his boots and pack and watched the quiet fire brighten as dark slipped down around the trees. The firelight bounced across the boulder on the far side of the brook where last spring a chipmunk had sat and eaten part of Daniel's sandwich. Was the chipmunk still alive? Or was he in the belly of a coyote or a hawk?

Seth climbed out of the lean-to to pee. Suddenly he was afraid. It was dark, dark. The big trees were tall shadows now. It seemed to Seth that they all were leaning down on him, as if to do him harm. And everywhere he looked he thought he saw creatures, strange, unknown creatures in the trees. They were watching him, watching him and waiting. He heard a stick crack off in the woods. Then right behind the lean-to, just a few feet away, there was a grinding, chewing sound.

He put more wood on the fire.

He was tired. It was time to sleep. He'd stay up to watch the fire just a little longer. He found himself staring at the firelight. It held him in a warm, bright circle, making a room of light for him, a place to live the night. And beyond that place, just a step away, there was the unknown dark, the wild and frightening dark.

Then a barred owl somewhere up on Dunn Hill began calling to the night. Seth could hear him saying, "Alone. Alone. Alone. A-l-o-n-e." Seth had always loved to hear owls calling in the night, but now that soft, round call made him feel even more lonely, even more afraid. The owl called again, "Alone. A-l-o-n-e."

Seth said to himself, almost in a whimper, "Me too."

Now Seth was fighting to stay awake. He added a couple of good-sized logs to the fire to make more

light. He was cold. He climbed, fully dressed, into his sleeping bag. The sleeping bag warmed him and made it even harder to stay awake. The owl called again. Then the moon rose, orange and huge, through the branches of the softwood trees. He fell asleep.

Sometime during the night, Seth didn't know exactly when, he awoke. The fire had died down to coals. Straight overhead, the black, bowl-like, cloudless sky held a full moon. Seth could see the moon's face, its eyes and nose, its round, open mouth.

The moon filled the woods with cold, silver light. It cast sharp black shadows everywhere. It lit the brook white. It was as if Seth had been carried away in a dream to another, unknown place, to an enormous, silent, black-and-white room, the lonely night-room of the earth. The world was still, as if it were dead. There was no wind, no sound, except the brook's quiet hiss.

Then somewhere between where Seth lay and his

warm house five miles to the east, a shrill, chilling cry rose over the earth. First one, then two, then three howls rising and falling, rising and falling. Then the short, sharp barks. Then the howls again. Coyotes. Then the answer came from somewhere behind him, nearby in the swamp.

Now Seth *wanted* to sleep. Sleep was the only place left to hide.

Quietly he crept out of the lean-to and added wood to the fire. He got back into his sleeping bag quickly. Then he lay back and listened to those unseen wanderers of the dark.

The next time Seth woke, the moon was down, and the sky toward the east was slowly turning pink. Now the forest was loud and alive again, filled to overflowing with the glad morning song of birds. The chickadee was singing, the myrtle warbler was singing, the junco and the cedar waxwing and a dozen other birds Seth couldn't recognize. They were all alive and singing in the dawn. Seth felt like singing too.

He climbed out of his sleeping bag, cold and happy. The rising sun washed away the last bits of night fear. He had made it! He made it through the night.

Seth started a new fire, then washed his face and rinsed his mouth in the cold water of the brook. For the first time Seth really understood why birds sing so joyously at dawn.

He had known all along that no harm would come to him in the night forest. He knew those coyotes were interested in mice, not people. But what his head knew and what his stomach felt were two very different things.

He chuckled to himself. Daniel had been right. A night in the forest wasn't at all like a night in the backyard. But he had done it, and he felt proud. No, pride wasn't exactly it. He just felt good, good about himself. He saw himself and the woods and its animals in a way he never had before.

Seth found a grub, caught a trout. Breakfast: one roast trout and a big pail of wintergreen tea. He found some cookie crumbs in the bottom of his pack and poured them in a neat pile on top of the boulder on the far side of the stream. Then he stepped around behind the lean-to and solved the mystery of last night's grinding, chewing sound. Here, at the base of a sugar maple tree, was a fresh, raw place where a porcupine had chewed away the bark.

When Seth returned to the lean-to, there was a chipmunk busily eating the cookie crumbs. Could it be the same chipmunk Seth had seen last spring? There was no way he could tell, but it was good to think it might be.

Seth rolled and packed the ground cloth and sleeping bag. He doused the fire, put away the salt and sugar, washed the tea pail, and hung it back on its nail.

When he was a few yards from the camp, he stopped and looked back. He felt alive, more alive than he ever had before. Then he laughed out loud and said, "I did it!"

Seth found a way around the waterfall and followed the brook through the abandoned pasture toward the road. He reached the road and headed home. It was another fine, bright day, clear and still. Seth sang softly to himself. He ambled down the road, loose in his bones.

David Budbill has been at various times a short-order cook, gardener, farm and woods laborer, carpenter's apprentice, and English teacher.

His poetry has been published in several anthologies and numerous periodicals. He has also written essays, plays, and a children's book, *Christmas Tree Farm.*

David Budbill, his wife, and son live in the mountains of northern Vermont.

Lorence F. Bjorklund has illustrated many books, among them *Cranes in My Corral* (Dial). He is particularly noted for his drawings of wildlife. Mr. Bjorklund lives in Croton Falls, New York.